BENJY'S BLANKET

by **MYRA BERRY BROWN**

pictures by **DOROTHY MARINO**

3   4   5

Library of Congress Catalog Card Number: 62-8427
Text © copyright 1962 by Myra Berry Brown
Illustrations © copyright 1962 by Franklin Watts, Inc.
Printed in the United States of America

BENJY'S BLANKET

Benjy was a little boy
who loved his baby blanket.
He'd had it for such a long time
it didn't look like a baby blanket any more —
it looked like a piece of rag.
But Benjy wanted to keep his blanket,
just the same.
He liked to hold it.
It was so soft.

Sometimes Benjy brought his blanket
with him to nursery school.
He held it
when he waved good-by to Mother
through the gate.

Once Benjy took his blanket along
to the barber shop.
He kept it on his lap
while the barber went "ZZZZZZZZ"
on the back of his neck.

Benjy needed his blanket
the first time he went
to the dentist.
He had to sit still
in the dentist's chair
and keep his mouth wide open
for a long time.
It was easier
if he could hold his blanket
while the dentist cleaned his teeth.

Most of all, Benjy liked to
hug his blanket
when he went to bed at night.

Not everybody understood about
Benjy and his blanket.
Trudy didn't. She lived next door.
She was older than Benjy.
She even had a loose tooth.
Trudy also had a brand-new baby kitten.
How that kitten meowed and meowed!

Benjy could tell that Trudy
didn't understand about his blanket.
She watched Benjy riding his tricycle.
"That blanket's going to get caught
in your wheels," Trudy said.

"It's so raggedy!
When are you going to throw it out?"
Benjy got *right off* his tricycle
and went inside his house.

Daddy was in his big chair
reading.
Daddy understood a little bit
about Benjy's blanket.
He asked Benjy,
"Aren't you ready to give up
that baby blanket yet?"
"Not yet," said Benjy.

Big brother Jim
didn't understand at all.
Jim was doing his homework.
He teased Benjy.
"Do you still have to
carry that old thing around?" he asked.
"Yes, I do," answered Benjy.

Mother understood.
She tucked Benjy into his new big boy's bed
and kissed him good night.
"Pretty soon you won't need
that blanket any more, Benjy."
"Pretty soon," said Benjy.
He closed his eyes.
He could still hear
Trudy's new kitten
meowing next door.

In the morning at breakfast, Daddy said,
"I wish Trudy could do something
about that kitten.
The meowing kept me awake half the night!'
"For heaven's sake," said Mother, "it's just a baby!"
"Dogs are much better," said big brother Jim.
Benjy listened and ate his cereal.

When Daddy went to work
Benjy stood on the front steps with his blanket
to wave good-by.

Trudy came out, too.
Daddy drove away.
He waved back from the car
and honked his horn.

That made Trudy's kitten meow.
"How's your kitty?" asked Benjy.

"He's right here. See?"
Trudy held up her kitten.
"He sure cries a lot," said Benjy.

Mother called from inside,
"Come and get your sweater, Benjy.
It's time to go to nursery school."

"You forgot your old blanket,"
yelled Trudy.
Sure enough, he had.
Benjy got it
and ran back into the house.

After school, Mother came for Benjy.
His teacher said, "Benjy was so brave today.
He climbed 'way to the top of the jungle gym."
"Benjy is growing up," said Mother.

Mother and Benjy walked out through the gate.
"Wait a minute," called the teacher.
"Benjy forgot his blanket."
She held it up high for Mother to see.

"Oh, dear," said Mother.
She waited while Benjy
ran back to get it.

Mother took Benjy to the shoe store
to buy new black shoes.
"You need a whole size larger," said the shoe man.
"Your feet are getting big!"

Benjy walked around the store
trying out his big new shoes.

Mother paid the shoe man.
Benjy carried the box himself.
He and Mother left the store.
The shoe man ran after them.
"Did your boy leave this?"
He held out Benjy's blanket.
"Oh, yes," said Mother. "Thank you."

Mother and Benjy went to market.
Benjy pushed the cart
around the store for Mother
and then up to the cash register.

"What a good boy!" said the lady.
She checked all of the groceries.
At the bottom of the cart
she found Benjy's blanket.
"Do you want this thing?"
"Thank you very much," said Mother.
Benjy took his blanket.

Walking home, Mother said,
"I wonder why you've been forgetting your blanket
everywhere today?"
Mother went into the house
with the marketing.
"I'm going next door to Trudy's," said Benjy.

Pretty soon Benjy ran into the kitchen.
Mother was cooking dinner.
"Back so soon?"
"The kitten's much better now," said Benjy.
"Is he?" said Mother.

"Come and see!"
Benjy pulled on Mother's apron.
"Just a minute," said Mother,
"while I cover the beans."

Trudy's back door was open.
Trudy and her mother
were looking down
into the basket on the floor.

"Your Benjy had the best idea!" said Trudy's mother.
"Benjy made my kitten stop crying!" said Trudy.
"The first time he's stopped meowing
in three days!" said Trudy's mother.
Benjy smiled.

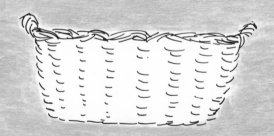

Mother looked into the basket.
"Why, Benjy!"
Mother put her arms around Benjy.
"How generous —
and how very grown-up!"
Mother turned to go back home.
"We'll have to tell Daddy about this!"

Mother came back with Daddy —
and big brother Jim, too.
Daddy looked into the basket and said,
"I don't believe it!"
Big brother Jim looked into the basket and said,
"Well, what do you know!"
Everyone was looking down
into the big basket.
There wasn't a sound
coming out of it.

Trudy's kitten was inside
curled up like a fluffy ball.
It wasn't sleeping.
It wasn't meowing.
Instead
it was wrapped in Benjy's baby blanket –
happy as a kitten could be.

Benjy felt very proud.
"That kitten was crying so much," he said,
"so I gave him my blanket.
He really needs it.
Besides, I'm a big boy now, you know."